MOONDANCE

A MOONBEAR *Book*

· FRANK ASCH ·

ALADDIN

NEW YORK   LONDON   TORONTO   SYDNEY   NEW DELHI

ALADDIN

An imprint of Simon & Schuster Children's Publishing Division

1230 Avenue of the Americas, New York, NY 10020

First Aladdin edition August 2014

Copyright © 1993 by Frank Asch

For information about special discounts for bulk purchases, please contact

Simon & Schuster Special Sales at 1-866-506-1949 or business@simonandschuster.com.

The Simon & Schuster Speakers Bureau can bring authors to your live event.

For more information or to book an event contact the Simon & Schuster Speakers Bureau

at 1-866-248-3049 or visit our website at www.simonspeakers.com.

Designed by Karina Granda

The text of this book was set in Olympian LT Std.

Manufactured in China 0614 SCP

10 9 8 7 6 5 4 3 2 1

Library of Congress Cataloging-in-Publication Data

Moondance / Frank Asch.

p. cm.

Summary: Bear fulfills his dream of dancing with the moon.

[1. Bears—Fiction. 2. Dance—Fiction. 3. Moon—Fiction.]

PZ7.A778Mpe   1993   [E]

92012358

ISBN 978-1-4424-6659-3 (hc)

ISBN 978-1-4424-6660-9 (pbk)

ISBN 978-1-4424-6661-6 (eBook)

To Devin

One night Bear and Little Bird were sitting outside, looking at the moon.

"You know what I wish?" said Bear. "I wish I could dance with the moon."

"Maybe she'd like to dance with you, too," chirped Little Bird.

Silly Bird," chuckled Bear. "The moon is so special. She wouldn't want to dance with me!"

Just then a cloud drifted in front of the moon.

"What about the clouds?" asked Little Bird. "Would they dance with you?"

"Mmmmmm . . . maybe," said Bear.

"Why don't you ask them," suggested Little Bird.

"Okay," said Bear, and he called to the clouds, "Clouds, would you come down and dance with me?"

But the clouds stayed up in the sky.

"You see," said Bear, "even the clouds won't come down to dance with me!"

Bear and Little Bird watched the sky until bedtime.

Then they said good night and went to sleep.

In the morning Bear looked out his window and saw fog. He had never seen fog before.

"Oh, my!" he cried. "The clouds came down to dance with me!"

Bear was so excited! He ran outside and began to dance with the clouds.

He danced and he danced and he danced.

As the day grew warmer, the fog began to lift.

When the fog was all gone, Bear felt sad.

"Do you think I could have stepped on their toes or something?" he asked Little Bird.

"Silly Bear," replied Little Bird. "The clouds probably had some work to do up high in the sky, that's all."

"What kind of work does a cloud do?" asked Bear.

"Clouds make rain," answered Little Bird.

Suddenly Bear had an idea.

"Clouds," he called to the sky, "could you make some rain for me to dance with?"

Bear heard no answer, not even a rumble of thunder.

"Oh well," he sighed. "I have my own work to do."

Bear forgot about the clouds.

He went inside and picked up his toys.

He washed the dishes and polished all the silverware.

When Bear was finished he looked out his window and saw raindrops falling from the sky.

"Oh, goodie!" cried Bear, and he ran outside and began to dance with the rain!

He danced and he danced and he danced.

After a while the rain stopped.

This time Bear was not sad.

"The rain got hungry and went home to eat supper, that's all," he said.

Bear was hungry too.

After eating *his* supper, Bear went outside and waited for the moon to rise.

For a long time Bear gazed at the moon.

She's so special and I'm just an ordinary bear, he thought.

Then Bear remembered how special it made him feel to dance with the clouds and the rain.

"Oh, Moon," he called to the sky, "will you please come down and dance with me?"

The moon made no reply, but when Bear looked down he saw the moon's reflection in a puddle.

"Look, Little Bird," he cried. "The moon came down to dance with me!"

Bear was so happy! He jumped into the puddle and began to dance with the moon.

He danced and he danced and he danced.